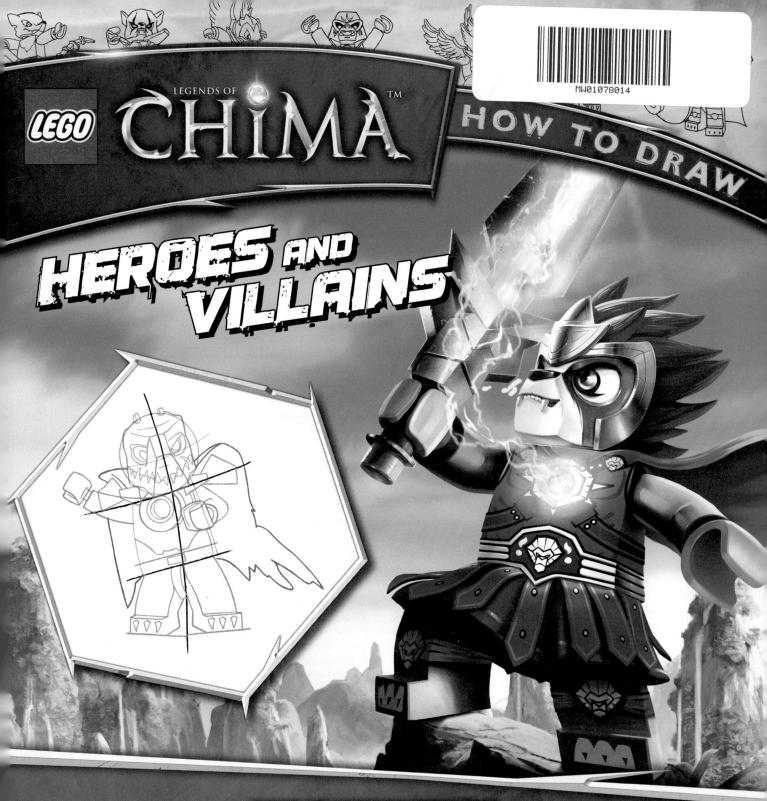

LEGO LEGENDS OF CHIMA™

HOW TO DRAW

HEROES AND VILLAINS

WRITTEN AND ILLUSTRATED BY RON ZALME

ISBN 978-0-545-64992-6

LEGO, the LEGO logo, the Brick and Knob configurations, the Minifigure and LEGENDS OF CHIMA are trademarks of the LEGO Group. ©2014 The LEGO Group. Produced by Scholastic Inc. under license from the LEGO Group.

Published by Scholastic Inc. SCHOLASTIC and associated logos are trademarks and/or registered trademarks of Scholastic Inc.

12 11 10 9 8 7 6 5 4 3 2 1   14 15 16 17 18/0

Printed in the U.S.A.   40

First Scholastic printing, January 2014

SCHOLASTIC INC.

UNLEASH THE POWER

Grab your pencil and get ready to CHI-up, because it's time to draw your favorite Legends of Chima™ characters! But before you begin, here are a few tools, tips, and tricks you'll need to bring your drawings to life:

What You'll Need

- ○ Basic #2 pencils.
- ○ Paper.
- ○ An eraser. *A "kneaded" eraser is best because it won't smudge.*
- ○ Rulers, circle guides, ellipse (oval) guides, and shaped curves. *Using these tools isn't cheating — they're necessary for smooth lines!*
- ○ Colored pencils, markers, or crayons for finishing touches. And a felt-tip pen is great for tracing over final lines.

Getting Started

In this book, you'll find line drawings of your favorite Chima characters broken down into easy-to-follow steps. Each drawing is labeled as ⊙, ⊙⊙, or ⊙⊙⊙ for **Easy**, **Medium**, or **Advanced**.

Each set of instructions begins with **foundation** lines drawn in black. These will help you place each part of your Chima character as you are sketching. New lines are added in blue for you to follow.

And remember: Practice makes perfect. Don't worry if your first drawings aren't just right. Keep at it, and they will get better and better!

The Shape of Things

When it comes to drawing your favorite Chima characters, they're really just made out of a few basic shapes. Take a look below to see the simple shapes that make up a basic Minifigure.

Tip!
For your first few drawings, consider tracing the basic shapes for each character to get started. As you grow more confident, try sketching them on your own.

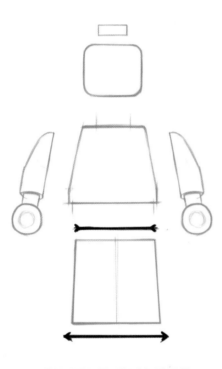

SIMPLE SHAPES

BASIC MINIFIGURE

3-D VIEW

SIDE VIEW

Now turn the page, and let's get drawing!

LAVAL

Laval is the headstrong prince of the Lion Tribe. He can be impulsive, which gets him into trouble. But with the help of his friends, Laval is learning to become a true leader and warrior.

Difficulty:

1

Start by drawing the three black foundation lines. Add a circle for Laval's head and a square for his body.

ARTIST'S TIP:
Use the large color images of the characters as guides for adding color to your own finished drawings!

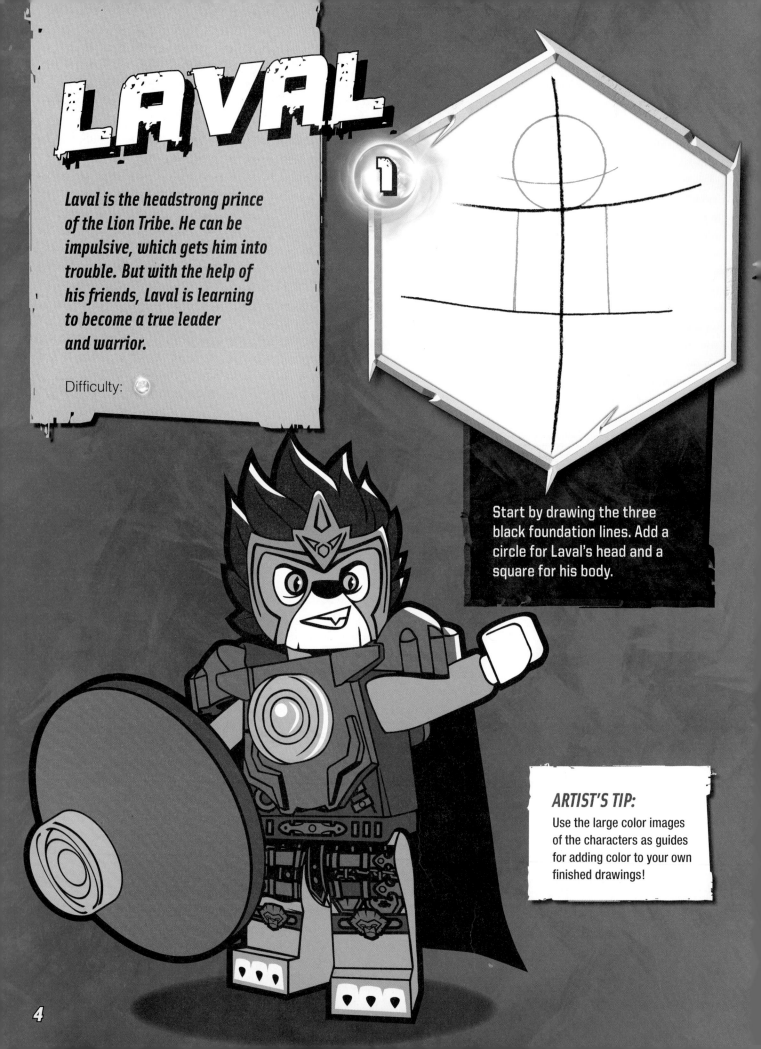

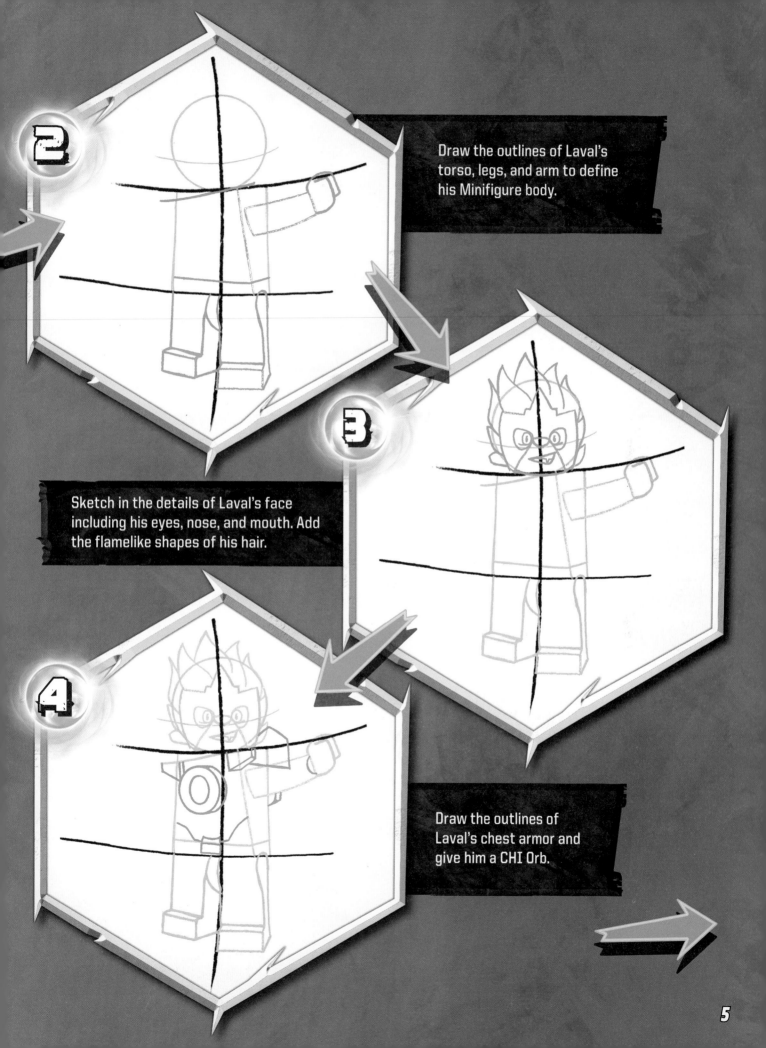

2

Draw the outlines of Laval's torso, legs, and arm to define his Minifigure body.

3

Sketch in the details of Laval's face including his eyes, nose, and mouth. Add the flamelike shapes of his hair.

4

Draw the outlines of Laval's chest armor and give him a CHI Orb.

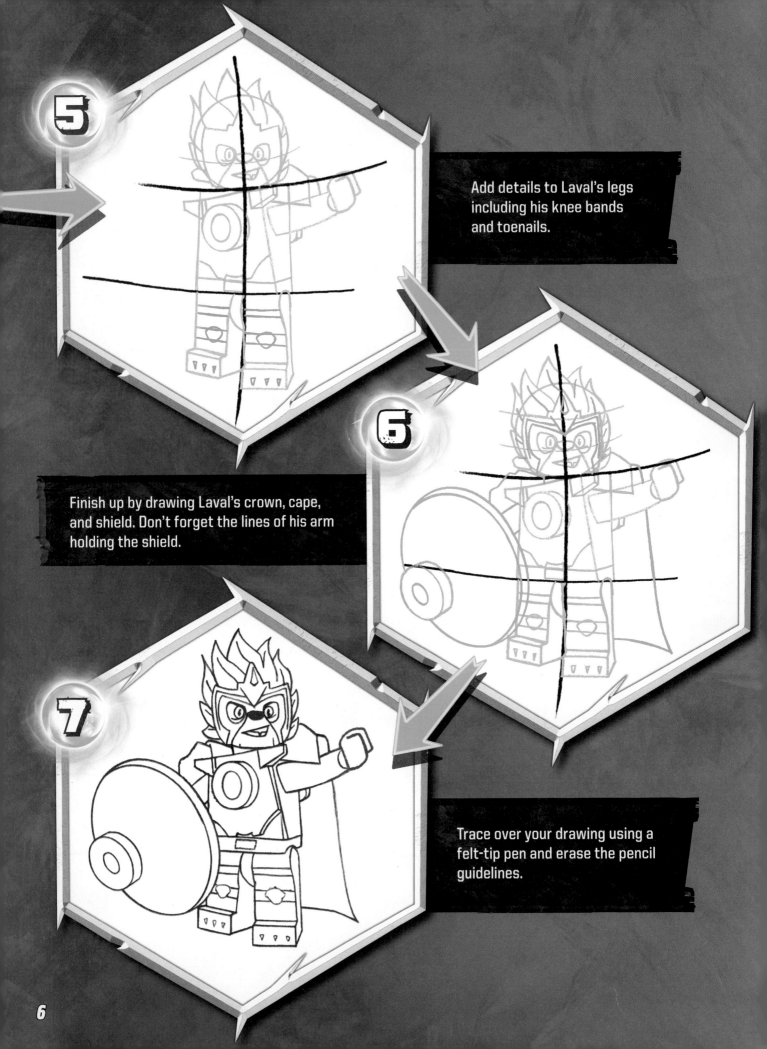

5

Add details to Laval's legs including his knee bands and toenails.

6

Finish up by drawing Laval's crown, cape, and shield. Don't forget the lines of his arm holding the shield.

7

Trace over your drawing using a felt-tip pen and erase the pencil guidelines.

CRAGGER

Cragger is the fierce leader of the Crocodile Tribe. He and Laval used to be best friends, but that was before the conflict over CHI began. Laval hopes that, one day, he can convince Cragger to stop fighting so they can be friends again.

Difficulty:

1

Start with three black foundation lines as shown. Draw a circle for Cragger's head and lightly sketch a guideline for his facial features. Add a square for his body.

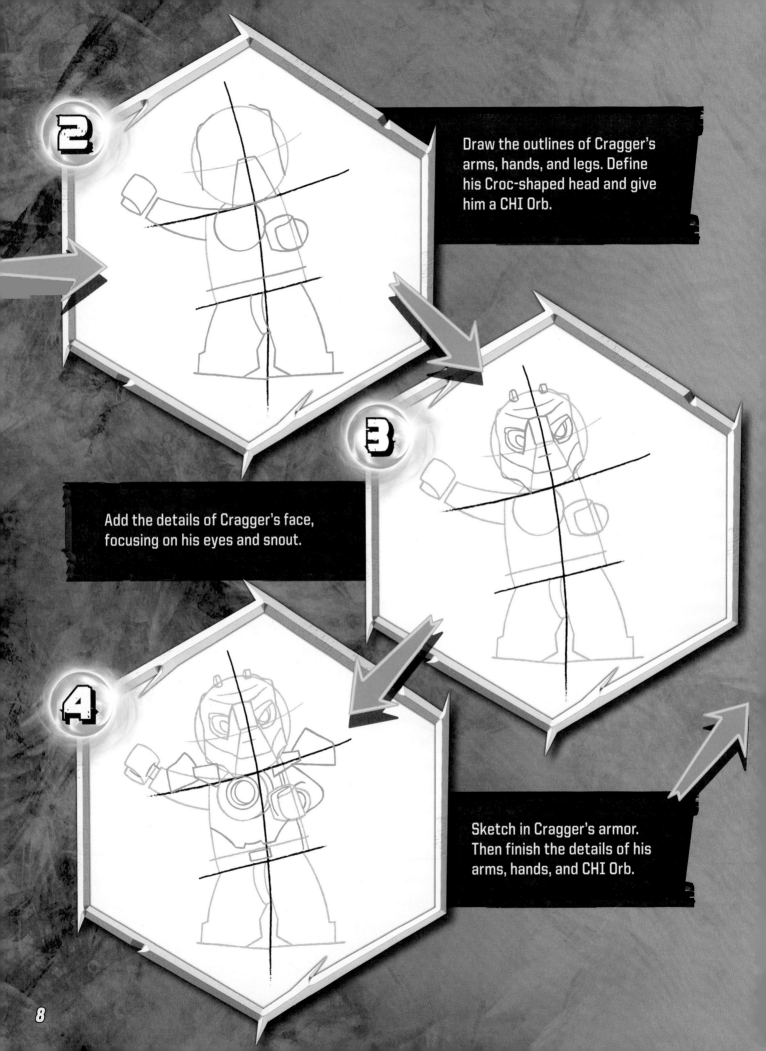

2

Draw the outlines of Cragger's arms, hands, and legs. Define his Croc-shaped head and give him a CHI Orb.

3

Add the details of Cragger's face, focusing on his eyes and snout.

4

Sketch in Cragger's armor. Then finish the details of his arms, hands, and CHI Orb.

5

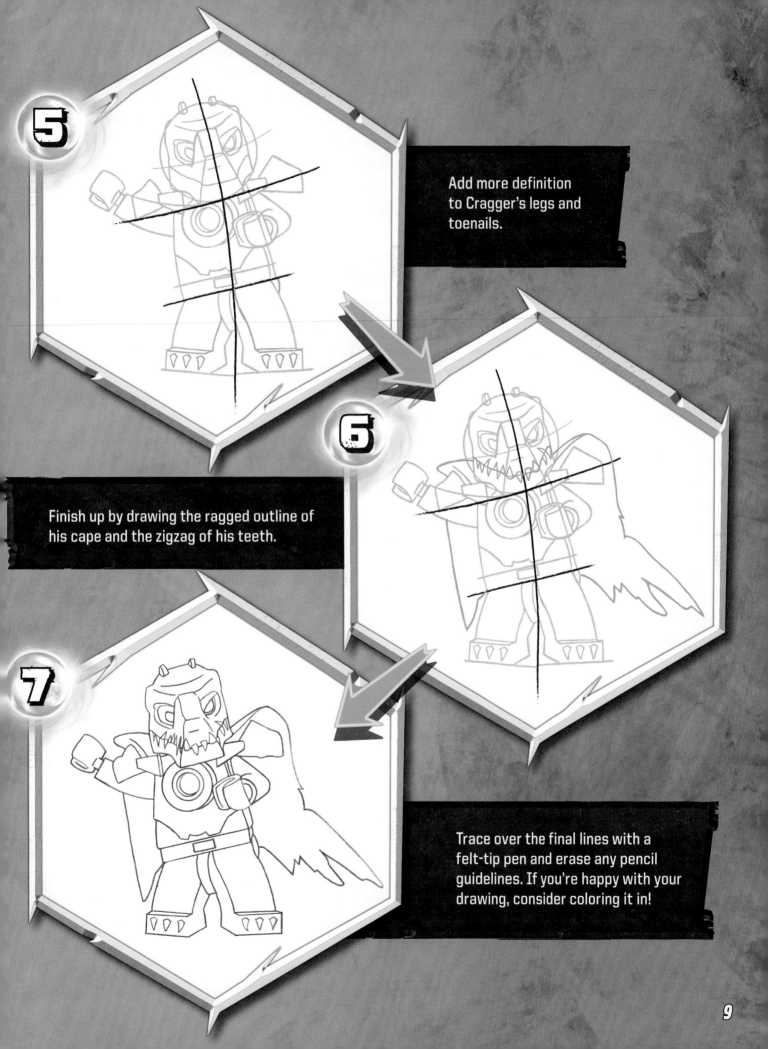

Add more definition to Cragger's legs and toenails.

6

Finish up by drawing the ragged outline of his cape and the zigzag of his teeth.

7

Trace over the final lines with a felt-tip pen and erase any pencil guidelines. If you're happy with your drawing, consider coloring it in!

RAZAR

Razar is one of the sneakiest Ravens in Chima. He's swindled every member of his tribe at least once, and they all admire him greatly for it! Every now and then he will use his skills at deception for the good of Chima—but only if the price is right.

Difficulty:

1

Draw the curved foundation lines as shown. Include a circle for Razar's head, a curved rectangle for his body, and a facial-features guideline.

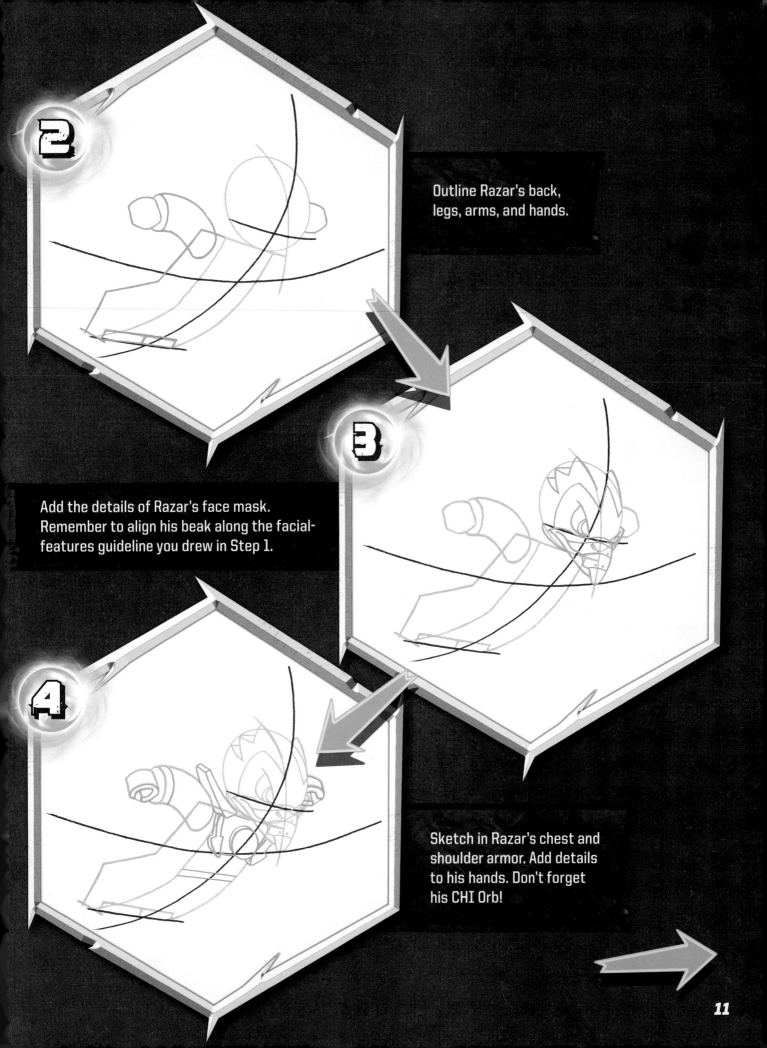

2

Outline Razar's back, legs, arms, and hands.

3

Add the details of Razar's face mask. Remember to align his beak along the facial-features guideline you drew in Step 1.

4

Sketch in Razar's chest and shoulder armor. Add details to his hands. Don't forget his CHI Orb!

5

Add the outlines of his legs and wings. Only draw simple, curved outlines for his wings for now. You'll add feathers in the next step.

6

Finish up by drawing in lots of feathers on Razar's wings.

7

Trace over the final lines with a felt-tip pen and erase the pencil sketch lines. Good work!

ERIS

Eris is the daughter of one of the Eagle Tribe's ruling council members. Unlike her fellow Eagles, who can sometimes be a bit scatterbrained, Eris is extremely quick-witted. Laval often trusts her for advice.

Difficulty: ● ● ●

1

Start by drawing three black foundation lines. Sketch a circle for her head, two curved lines for the side of her body, and a facial-features guideline.

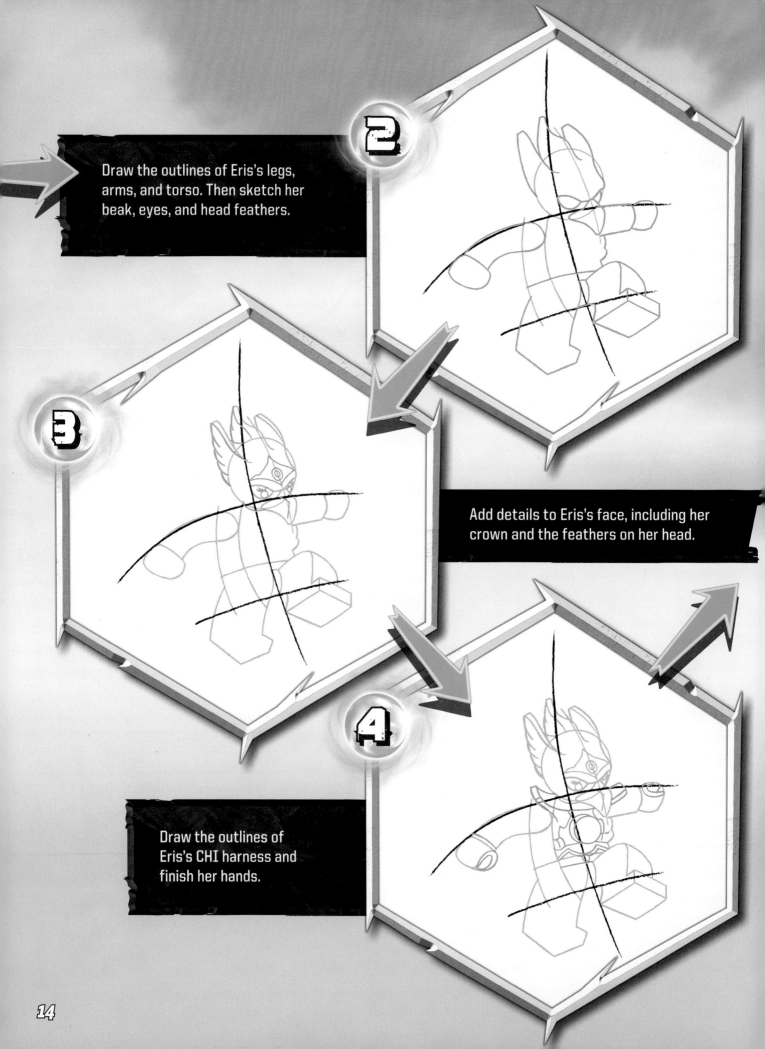

2

Draw the outlines of Eris's legs, arms, and torso. Then sketch her beak, eyes, and head feathers.

3

Add details to Eris's face, including her crown and the feathers on her head.

4

Draw the outlines of Eris's CHI harness and finish her hands.

5

Sketch the details of Eris's legs and add the outlines of her wings.

6

Carefully draw the two layers of feathers on Eris's wings as shown.

7

Eris is now complete! Compare your drawing to the final version and make changes if you like. Finish by tracing over your drawing with a felt-tip pen.

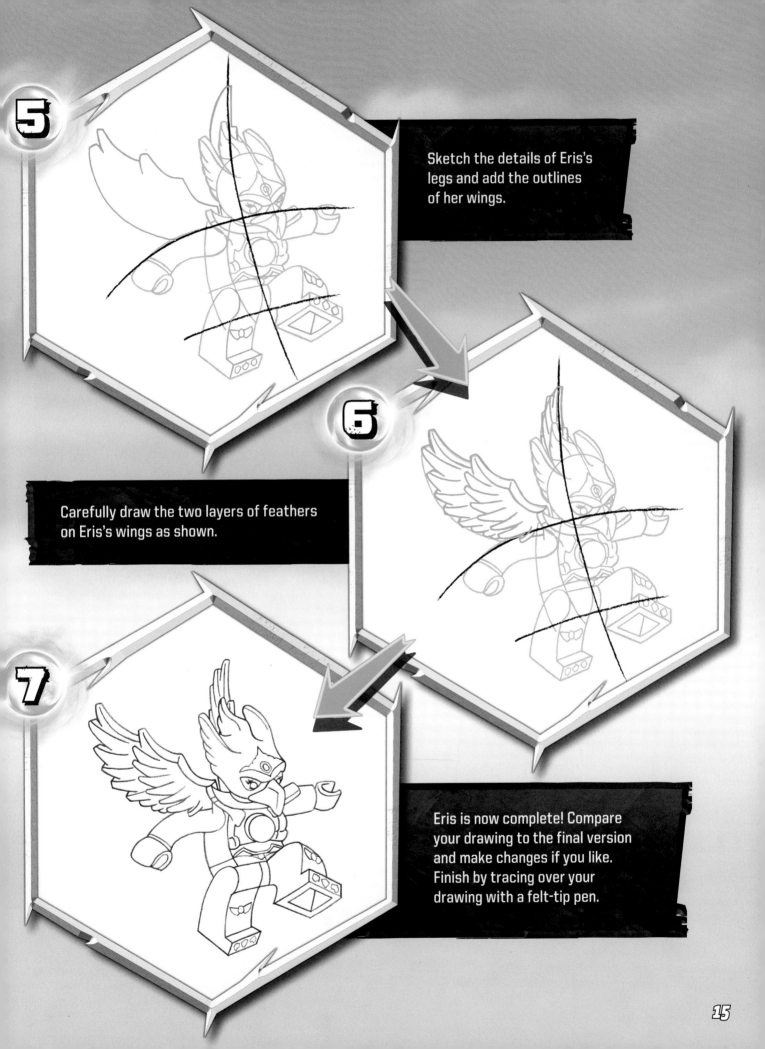

FURTY

Furty, short for Furtivo, is a sly Fox who is one of the few animals in Chima without a tribe. He is distantly related to the Wolves, but couldn't be more different from them. While the Wolves always look out for one another, Furty only looks out for himself.

Difficulty:

2

Finish sketching Furty's legs. Draw his ears and snout.

1

Start with three foundation lines. Add ovals for Furty's head and tail. Then outline his torso, arms, and hands.

3

Add details to Furty's face including his eyes and teeth.

4

Finish the detail lines of his torso, hands, and toenails. Then add fur to his tail.

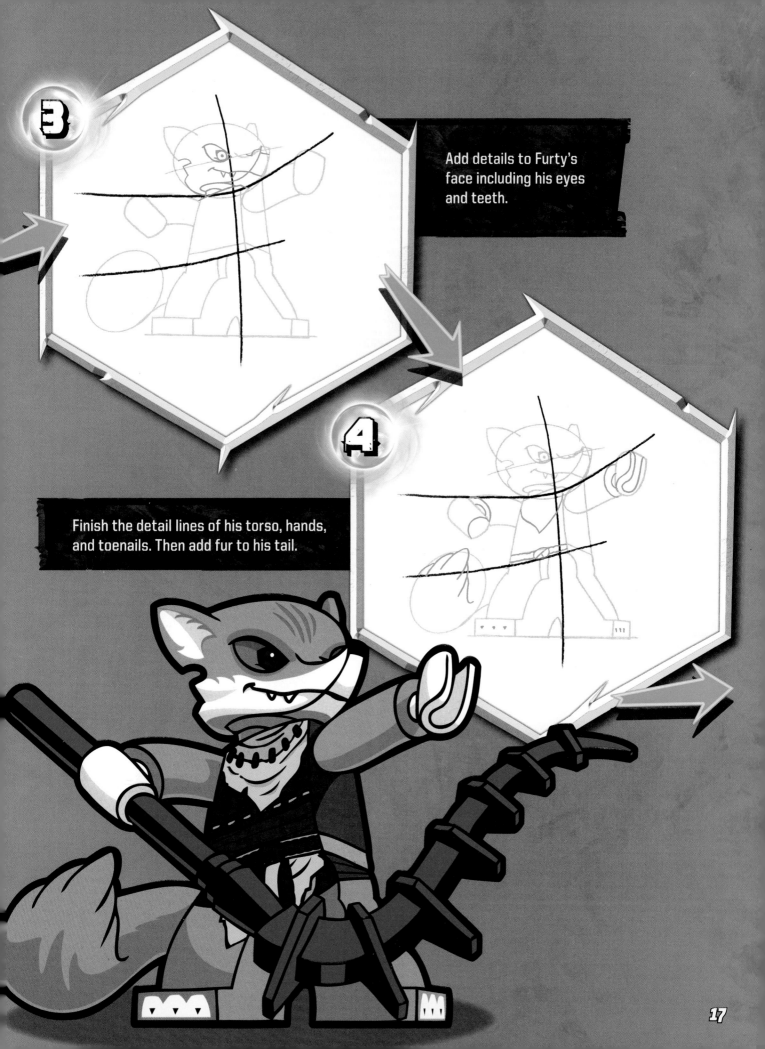

5 It's time to draw Furty's whip-like weapon. Start with a long cylinder for the handle. Then draw the curved *S* shape as shown for the whip.

6 Study the example carefully and add the 3-D blades along Furty's weapon.

7 Clean up your artwork and darken the final lines. If you're happy with your drawing, try coloring it to match the large image of Furty on page 17.

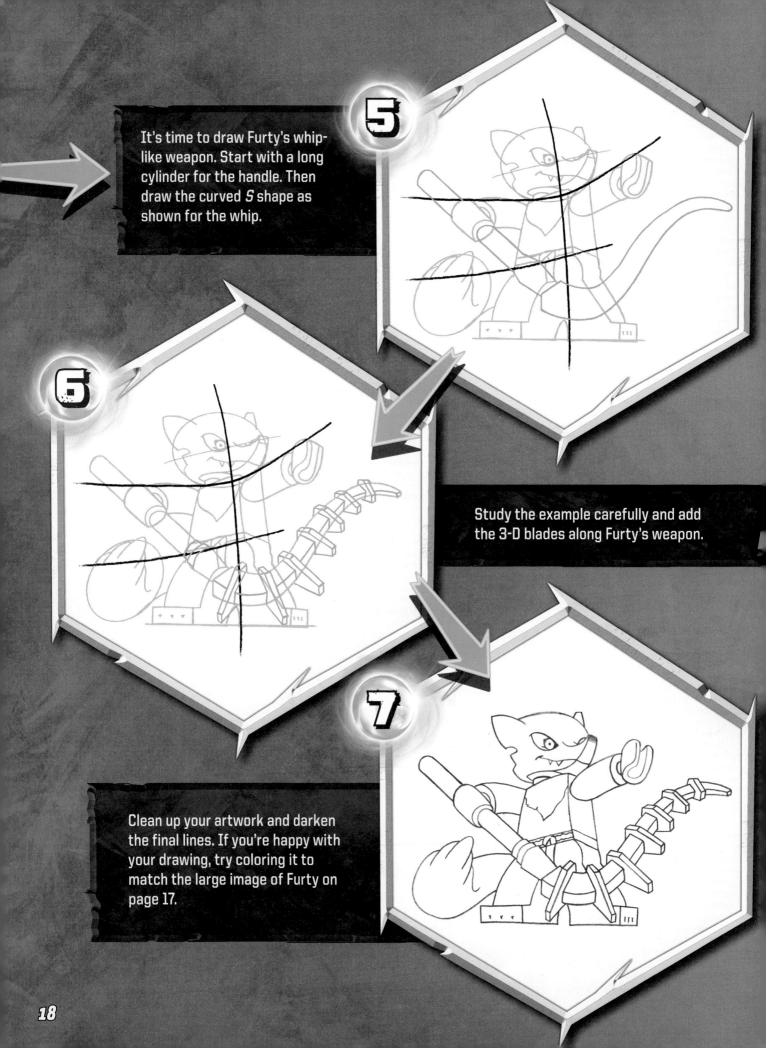

GORZAN

Despite his fierce appearance, Gorzan the Gorilla is a peaceful, nature-loving creature. He'd much rather meditate than fight. But when the safety of Chima is at stake, watch out. This warrior won't hesitate to show his might!

Difficulty:

1

Draw three black foundation lines. Sketch a circle for Gorzan's head and two ovals for his hands. Add lines to mark his knees, feet, and torso. Add a facial-features guideline.

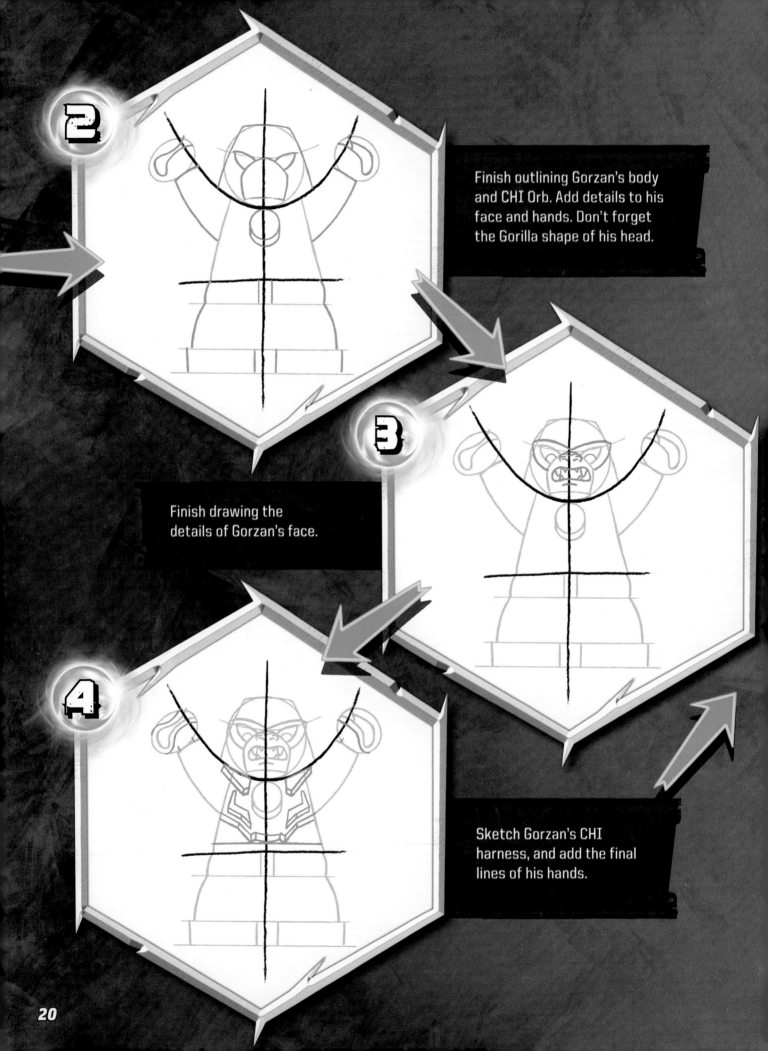

2

Finish outlining Gorzan's body and CHI Orb. Add details to his face and hands. Don't forget the Gorilla shape of his head.

3

Finish drawing the details of Gorzan's face.

4

Sketch Gorzan's CHI harness, and add the final lines of his hands.

5

Draw Gorzan's knee bands and waistcloth.

6

Finish by adding in Gorzan's face paint and giant toenails.

7

Trace over your final lines with a felt-tip pen and erase the guidelines. Great job!

GRIZZAM

Grizzam is the only white Gorilla member in his tribe. This sometimes makes him feel like a loner, but then he remembers that in the Great Mellow, everyone is unique for a reason.

Difficulty:

2

Sketch three boxlike shapes as shown for Grizzam's hands and foot.

1

Start with three foundation lines. Add a circle for Grizzam's head and two crossed facial-feature guidelines. Draw the curve of his back.

3

Add the details of Grizzam's face, including his eyes, nose, mouth, and the pointy shape of his head.

4

Move on to Grizzam's torso by sketching the lines of his shoulder, chest, collar, and CHI harness. Draw in his other foot.

5

It's time to add details. Draw the claw shapes of Grizzam's oversized gloves and add finger lines and knobs. Draw the details of his shoulder armor.

6

Finish up with Grizzam's feet, toenails, knee pads, and the 3-D box shape on the bottom of his foot.

7

Clean up your sketch and erase any unwanted lines. Consider adding a background to bring your drawing to life, like a vine for Grizzam to swing on!

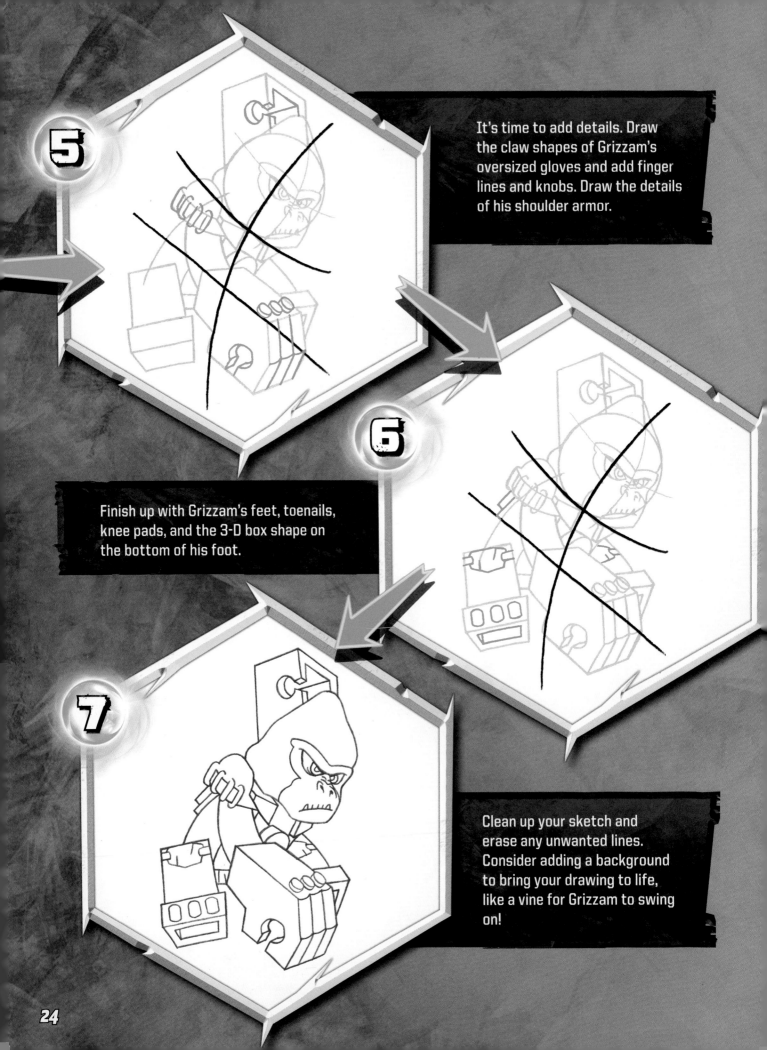

SKINNET

Skinnet is a very friendly, enthusiastic Skunk. The only problem is he smells really bad. So it's hard for him to make friends. Laval and Eris always try to be nice to him, but it helps if they bring nose plugs.

Difficulty:

1

ARTIST'S TIP:
Follow the first four enlarged steps to draw Skinnet's body. Then follow Steps 5 and 6, which are zoomed out, to draw his spear.

Draw two foundation lines. Start with two ovals for Skinnet's head and tail. Add lines to mark his torso and legs. Draw a long line for his spear.

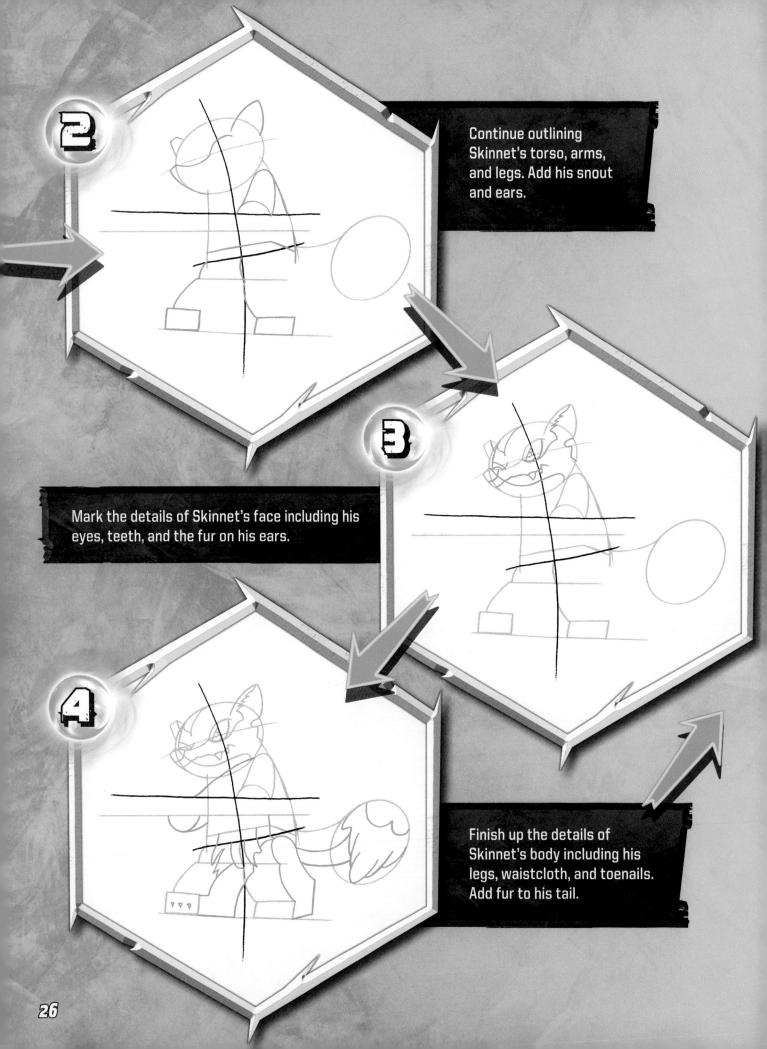

2

Continue outlining Skinnet's torso, arms, and legs. Add his snout and ears.

3

Mark the details of Skinnet's face including his eyes, teeth, and the fur on his ears.

4

Finish up the details of Skinnet's body including his legs, waistcloth, and toenails. Add fur to his tail.

5

Sketch Skinnet's hands holding the weapon and draw the point of his spear.

6

Finish up by drawing a leaf on Skinnet's spear as shown.

7

All done! Clean up your drawing and consider coloring it. Or maybe draw a stink cloud behind him?

WORRIZ

Worriz is the ruthless leader of the Wolf Tribe. Though he is gruff toward outsiders, he is always extremely loyal to his tribe. Worriz also has a keen ability to sense danger and, like any Wolf, he is a master of strategy.

Difficulty:

1

Start with three black foundation lines. Draw a circle for Worriz's head and two ovals for his hands. Mark lines for his torso and legs.

ARTIST'S TIP:
If you're particularly happy with a drawing, try photocopying it so you can color it in with different details. That way, you won't mess up your original in case you want to color it a different way.

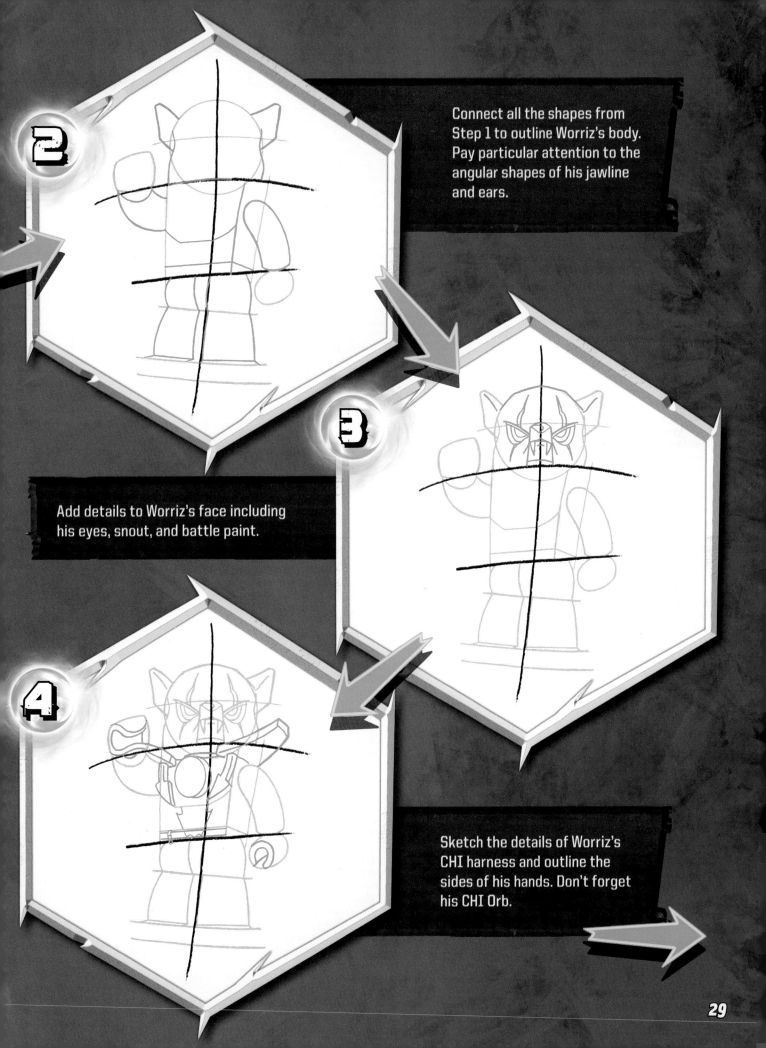

2

Connect all the shapes from Step 1 to outline Worriz's body. Pay particular attention to the angular shapes of his jawline and ears.

3

Add details to Worriz's face including his eyes, snout, and battle paint.

4

Sketch the details of Worriz's CHI harness and outline the sides of his hands. Don't forget his CHI Orb.

5

Finish up Worriz's legs with knee wraps and toenails. Add the fur decoration on his belt.

6

Draw the ragged outline of Worriz's cape to complete your sketch.

7

That's it! Clean up your drawing and darken the lines you want to keep. Why not make up a weapon or two for Worriz to hold?

CRUG

Crug is Cragger's lead Crocodile thug. He is pure muscle — big, strong, and blindly obedient. Still, Crug has a soft side. Rumor has it he sleeps with a stuffed frog named Mr. Flipper-Lovey.

Difficulty:

1

Start with three foundation lines. Draw a circle for Crug's head and lines for his torso and feet.

Outline Crug's arms, hands, and legs. Draw his curved jawline, the ridges on his head, and his eye.

2

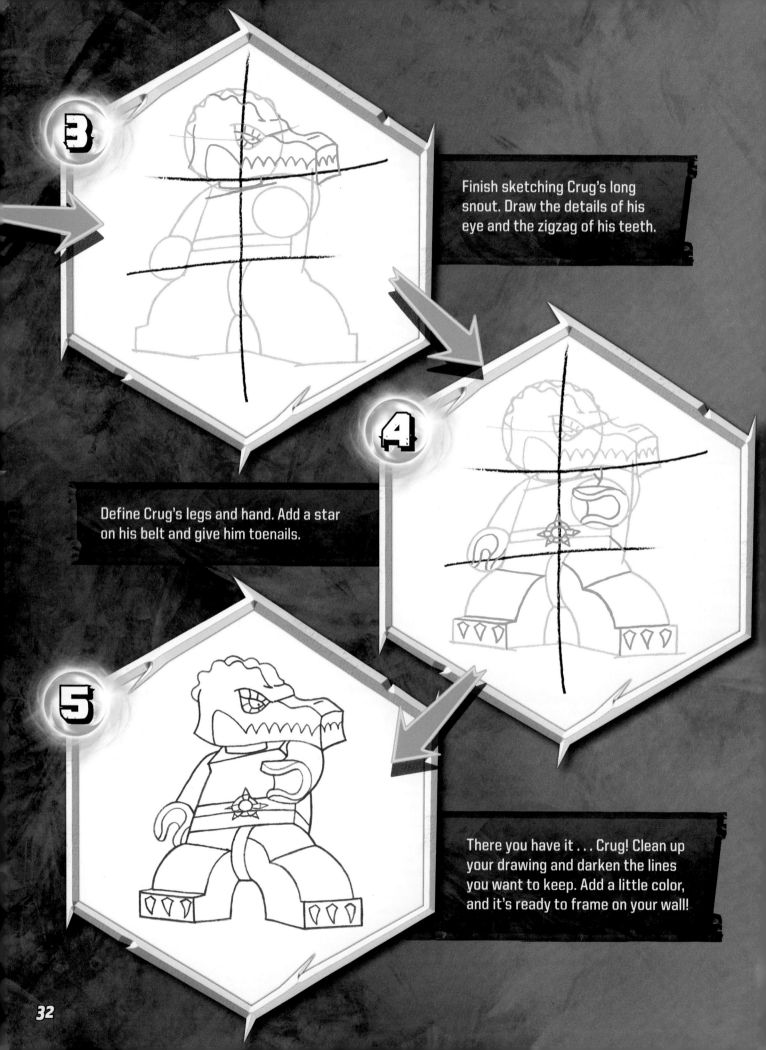

3

Finish sketching Crug's long snout. Draw the details of his eye and the zigzag of his teeth.

Define Crug's legs and hand. Add a star on his belt and give him toenails.

4

5

There you have it . . . Crug! Clean up your drawing and darken the lines you want to keep. Add a little color, and it's ready to frame on your wall!